Short Horror Stories

Shacklebound Books Drabble Anthologies

Eric Fomley

Published by Shacklebound Books, 2022.

SHORT HORROR STORIES

First edition. October 18, 2022.

ISBN: 979-8215336649

Written by Eric Fomley.

Table of Contents

For Cassy, my better half.

Also by Shacklebound Books

Shacklebound Books Drabble Anthologies
Drabbledark: An Anthology of Dark Drabbles
Drabbledark II: An Anthology of Dark Drabbles
Chronos: An Anthology of Time Drabbles
Wyrms: An Anthology of Dragon Drabbles

Shacklebound Books Flash Fiction Anthologies
Timeshift: Tales of Time
Sins and Other Worlds
Maelstroms
Dread Space
The Mods

Other Drabble Publications
Martian: Year One
Dystopia Drabble Showcase

SFF Excursions
War Torn
War Pawns

Pre-Mortem Photography
Taylor Rae

Hold still. I can't cut you yet.

I always shave the men. Your faces look so agonized, innocent.

Relax. That injection earlier, in my van? That's succinylcholine. Neuromuscular-blocker. It's already paralyzing you, nerve by nerve.

The Victorians posed their dead with wires, like I've done to you. Their post-mortem photos are the clearest. Nobody living sits that still.

Nobody except you.

You're the perfect subject. Only the blood will show which picture is post-mortem.

Look at the camera. It's antique. Victorian, in fact. Your delicious fear will be frozen, mine forever.

Don't cry. I'd hate to ruin a good photo.

TAYLOR RAE's work has appeared with *Flash Fiction Online, NYC Midnight,* and *Pseudopod.* For more, check out www.mostlytaylor.com

Finders Keepers
Alyson Tait

There're no children laughing deep in the forest. No dogs or cats wander down the street.

In fact, the streets stop about a dozen miles from the witch's house. There's no room for cars, no footpath to help you get there.

There's no footpath to show you how to get back out – and that is no mistake on the part of the witch. She does so like her privacy.

She doesn't like her rare visitors to leave, either. Once you find the witch's house, buried so deep inside the woods, you and all your bones will likely be permanent guests.

ALYSON TAIT has appeared in *(mac)ro(mic)* and *Wrongdoing Magazine*, among others. You can find her on Twitter @rudexvirus1 or at AlysonTait.com.

The Small Town Dead
Dorian J. Sinnott

There was no warning when townsfolk started dropping dead. At first, it was the neighbors. And then the butcher. The banker. The baker.

Dead. Without reason.

All were healthy. So alive just days before. We couldn't make sense of it—simply fear who would be next. *If* we would be next. A cruel lottery.

It was only when they were to be buried that deep dread set in.

The cemetery had been dug up—graves empty. Yet, looming in the distance, there they stood. Reanimated. Rotting corpses stretching in the morning sun.

The dead lived on, as the living died.

DORIAN J. SINNOTT's word has appeared in over 200 journals and has been nominated for the Best of the Net. Find him on Twitter @doriansinnott

An Incomplete List of Things that Give Me Diarrhea

Jason P. Burnham

Milk
Ice cream
Soft cheeses
Dairy products generally, except somehow frozen yogurt
Peanuts
Almonds
Cashews
Other nuts and pseudo-nuts, though I can't always differentiate nut, fruit, or bud, nor do I care to try each and every one to figure it out
Extremely spicy foods
Anything if I eat it too soon after a vigorous exercise session

"This isn't exactly what we had in mind when we asked if you had any last words," said the executioner.

Sonya smiled. "And humans," she finished, then unhinged her jaw and swallowed every human in the room. She knew she'd regret it later.

JASON P. BURNHAM has his fair share of food allergies.
Twitter: @AndGalen

Aftershocks

L.V. Rose

The night it happened, a spider studied us from its web in the safe little corner above the cement stairs.

Now, in my dreams, crawling stipple-gray bodies scramble up the soft flesh of my calves. A writhing, skittering horde necklaces my throat and pries open my mouth, scratching the surface of my tongue with hungry spindle fingers.

Each time I wake, they wash away. Maybe if I told someone, the spiders would leave me alone. Maybe if I screamed, they would erupt from my veins like ink.

I look in the mirror and spit black slivers into the bathroom sink.

L.V. ROSE is an editor, educator, and emerging author who writes about monsters both real and imagined. @WordsRose

Escape
Rachel L. Tilley

I shout, but no sound comes. I bang on the coffin lid, but the noise is drowned out by the revelries above. I am not interred in a cemetery – below someone's house, perhaps?

My blind panic crescendos in unison with my heart's beating.

Except... as morning approaches, I remember. It *isn't* beating. Each full moon, my soul returns to Earth; to this same accursed spot. My body, once stolen and buried alive, is long since decayed and gone.

Now they dance over my grave, oblivious to the horrors below.

Yet, night-time is a blessing compared to what the dawn brings.

RACHEL L. TILLEY, who lives in the UK, writes short stories in the fantasy and horror genres. www.instagram.com/rachel_l_tilley

Scrapple
Warren Benedetto

"I'll have the scrapple," I said.

The waitress glanced at the fist-sized bruise on my arm, then at Mike. I nodded. She jotted on her pad.

"Coffee." Mike thrust the menu at the waitress. "Black."

The waitress disappeared into the kitchen. Through the swinging doors, I saw her hand my order to the cook. He read it, then looked out at me. Eye contact. A small nod.

"What's even in scrapple?" Mike sneered.

"Pork bits," I explained. "Lips, nips, and assholes."

The cook emerged from the kitchen. He approached Mike from behind, meat cleaver in hand.

"Mostly assholes," I added.

"Scrapple" was originally published in Dark Moments by Black Hare Press in April 2021.

WARREN BENEDETTO writes short fiction about horrible people doing horrible things. Visit www.warrenbenedetto.com and follow @warrenbenedetto on Twitter.

Memento Mori
Edward Ahern

Most cemeteries are forgettable, with identical slabs spaced rigorously on grass. Living mourners visit less and less frequently, and memories of the dead dissipate long before the lettering is weathered unreadable.

Once the living have forgotten their dead, the dead nurture their own. Unphysical things sprout in the estates of the moldered, reaching into the miasmas of night. Speech has rotted away with lungs, and as they sway in darkness their intercourse is twisted-wind wailings and a semaphore of ghost lights. The living are unwelcome, for the dead wish to talk only among themselves, and the dead know their own.

ED AHERN's had over three hundred stories and poems published so far, and six books. He edits at *Bewildering Stories*.

Suzie May's Garden
Dorian J. Sinnott

Suzie May had the most beautiful garden in town. Every spring, the flowers would blossom—a botanical sea of fuchsias and golds. Pansies and daffodils. Tulips and daisies. All so prim. So perfect.

She claimed she had good fertilizer. Made fresh from her farming of putrid earthworms. I'd seen her out there at night, near the tent she raised them. Humming beneath the milk light of moon. Watching as they churned in the soil. Fresh for planting.

I never questioned it, until her dog started bringing over bones. Rooted out from the tent. Covered in the stench of the earthworms.

DORIAN J. SINNOTT's word has appeared in over 200 journals and has been nominated for the Best of the Net. Find him on Twitter @doriansinnott

Shipwrecked
DJ Tyrer

Spluttering, he scrambled his way out of the water and up the beach. A surge of relief filled him that he'd survived. The sole survivor.

Just a short distance above the tidal line, he found the skeleton slumped against a tree. On its wrist, a watch, the same make as his own.

Crouching, he looked closely at it. The time it stopped – the moment the ship sank. He checked his own: the same.

Tearing it from the bony wrist, he sought the inscription: To him from his wife.

Recoiling, he looked wildly about, seeking escape, yet knowing there was none.

"Shipwrecked" was originally published in Siren's Call issue 48 (December 2019).

DJ TYRER runs *Atlantean Publishing*, and has had flash fiction published in *Sirens Call*, *Tigershark*, and on *Trembling With Fear*.

https://djtyrer.blogspot.co.uk/
https://www.facebook.com/DJTyrerwriter/

Old Jasper
Marc Sorondo

I figured it was a local myth...nothing more.

I'd heard the stories. A guy lost a hand in the thirties. Kids who'd gone swimming in Lake Jasper back in the forties and fifties when that was still allowed who'd never come back, cause of death listed as drowning but bodies never recovered.

Every town had their haunted houses and spooky roads, and I believed this no different.

Then I took my dog for a walk along the lake and a snapping turtle the size of a Volkswagen Beetle lunged out of the water and snapped Booker's head clean off.

MARC SORONDO lives with his wife and children. He's a perpetual student and occasional teacher. Check out MarcSorondo.com.

Her Eyes
Alyson Tait

Originally, her eyes were painted on, acrylic filling in that vital part of her face.

I think this was a most vital mistake.

Her painted-on eyes created an opening. Had the artist painted on a blindfold instead, perhaps the devil would've been kept at bay just this once.

Tonight, her eyes are flesh and blood. They roam around the room, trying to find me again. They search the shadows, and I watch as they squint to see under the bed. Her eyes may have become real, but lucky for me; the rest of her is still stiff and mostly porcelain.

ALYSON TAIT has appeared in *(mac)ro(mic)* and *Wrongdoing Magazine*, among others. You can find her on Twitter @rudexvirus1 or at AlysonTait.com.

There'll Be No Peace Tonight
Geraldine Borella

A drop of water. That's how it starts.

It falls from the trophy room ceiling—seepage from a burst pipe above—and lands on the shrivelled up vine-girl.

Upstairs, the hunter sleeps, submerged in his favourite dream—of chasing her, catching her, pulling her up by the roots.

The drop now a trickle, shoots begin to sprout. Fresh tendrils unfurl and spear into the soil of a houseplant. A peace lily, of all things.

Planting roots, the vine-girl grows—in strength and fury—then twirls her sinuous arms around the staircase balustrades and snakes her way into the hunter's room.

GERALDINE BORELLA writes speculative fiction published by *Deadset Press, IFWG Publishing,*

AHWA/Midnight Echo. To find out more, go to https://geraldineborella.com/about/

Death Gods Rising
Hazel Ragaire

Survive. Survive beneath millennia of permafrost soil. In darkness we wait. Warmth's tendrils tease by degrees and our cage cracks. Long-dormant bacteria yawn, embracing oxygen. We wiggle, yearning for hosts. Viral Sleeping Beauties will seek canvases for pain and pustules, painting pliable flesh with brilliant reds.

Above, we are extinct; no record of our conquests remain. We are death gods, coming. Life and evolution's architects. We are not without mercy; you may prepare.

We will reap the land, bringing balance. My kin will burn or shrivel or suffer petri dishes. But some will sink back to darkness and thrive. Waiting.

"Death Gods Rising" originally appeared in Beneath published by Ghost Orchid Press.

HAZEL RAGAIRE breathes life into monster monstrosities and weird stories sprinkling sci-fi and fantasy everywhere: @HRagaire or www.hazelragaire.com.

Prone to Misinterpretation
John H. Dromey

Multiple axe murder victims were discovered in a cellar room filled with body fluids and parts. How deep was the pile of blood and guts? The first detective on the scene found himself up to his neck in gore after he slipped on the slick floor.

Unfortunately, his forehead scraped the edge of the discarded murder weapon, and he added fresh blood to the mix. He lost consciousness.

The detective awoke in complete darkness. Suffocating. His oxygen-starved limbs refused to move. Worse still, he could not summon enough breath to call for help in getting out of the body bag.

"Prone to Misinterpretation" by John H. Dromey was first published in Trembling With Fear (2019).

JOHN H. DROMEY enjoys reading—mysteries in particular—and writing in a variety of genres.

Her Garden
Gully Novaro

One year sober. One year since she left.

One year since I woke up to a messy house and an empty bed. To a gash on my head and a broken bottle.

I looked out for her garden, for the plants she had cared for, but my thumbs were anything but green. Soon, the whole field had died on me, except for the tomatoes.

The tomatoes grew bloody red and plump. I picked one and cut into it today. Something hard stopped the knife in its tracks.

Found a ring on a boney finger, and memories I had left behind.

GULLY NOVARO is a non-binary writer from Argentina, with love for all things out of this world.

Eyes of Mine
Rachel L. Tilley

Your eyes remind me of emeralds.

Your first girlfriend wore emeralds. They provoke me.

I can't help but picture all those other gems of yours. Things I never had, but endlessly coveted.

You may have expelled me from your school of artistry, but you inspire me to craft and create nonetheless; I'm still your devoted pupil, brother.

It's like staring at my own reflection. Perhaps I'll take your place as teacher when you're... gone.

We're virtually identical.

Except.

Baby moonstones drip like tears.

A bruise on your left cheek, reveals a glistening amethyst.

Soon, I will make you bleed rubies.

RACHEL L. TILLEY, who lives in the UK, writes short stories in the fantasy and horror genres. www.instagram.com/rachel_l_tilley

For Our First Date I Wear Red
Addison Smith

The body screams as I wrest control from its owner, possessing him once again. I pull his hands from his chest and they come away red and clotted. I examine him in the bathroom mirror and smile, though it does not touch the body's eyes. A heart is carved jagged across his chest. I imagine his hands shaking as the knife dug into his skin, not under his control or mine, but that of another. Is this what they call a meet-cute? I retrieve a knife from the floor and begin a message to the other who possesses this body.

ADDISON SMITH writes weird science fiction, fantasy, and horror. His stories have appeared in *Fantasy Magazine, Fireside Magazine,* and others.

The Enemy Within
Toshiya Kamei

I stroll past walls lined with coffin-like capsules cradling astronauts in fitful slumbers. Their dreams flicker on the monitors next to the capsules. Some dreams appear harmless, at least initially. On horseback, Captain Rodríguez dashes across a broad green meadow. With a shrieking neigh, the horse comes to a sudden halt and throws its rider to the ground. Rodríguez lands on his head, convulses, and stops moving. I sneer as he flatlines. Others, sheer nightmares from the get-go. Sargent Yamamoto's face contorts. My own face looms large on her screen. She lets out a silent scream. I disconnect her tubes.

"The Enemy Within" was originally published in Hundred Word Horror: Cosmos in May 2021.

TOSHIYA KAMEI writes short fiction inspired by mythology, folklore, and fairy tales.

Curiosity Kills
Warren Benedetto

On the first day, the cat brought me a mouse and laid it on my doorstep, teeth marks oozing through its dust-gray fur.

On the second day, the cat brought me a red-breasted robin and left it on my kitchen table, blood-splattered and broken-winged next to my blueberry muffin.

On the third day, the cat brought me a rabbit and dropped it at my feet while I brushed my teeth, its innards oozing like cranberry sauce through a gash torn through its belly.

Today, I woke up to the sound of a newborn baby crying.

I don't have a baby.

"Curiosity Kills" was originally published in the Extreme Drabbles of Dread anthology by Macabre Ladies Publishing in Dec 2020.

WARREN BENEDETTO writes short fiction about horrible people doing horrible things. Visit www.warrenbenedetto.com and follow @warrenbenedetto on Twitter.

Soulmates
Kailey Alessi

I knew we were meant to be the moment I saw you. Your obsidian hair, cornflower blue eyes, soft lips stole my breath away, even from a distance. You and I were meant to be.

I know you don't see that now, but you will. Someday you'll know that I am right. That we're connected. Soulmates, fated by the very stars to be together.

But for now, you're still confused, and I have to make sure that you don't do anything rash. The chains are just temporary, my love, I promise. Just until you realize that you love me too.

KAILEY ALESSI has lived in Michigan and Idaho. An anthropology graduate student by day, by night she writes disturbing fiction.

Old Woman of Willow Wood
Dana Vickerson

"Dare," I say, and their eyes go wide. I'd rather do whatever Jenny can come up with than tell her the truth about anything.

Jenny smirks and twirls her marshmallow. "I dare you to call the old woman."

I scoff. "Piece of cake."

I walk through the drooping willow branches, parting them like hanging beads, and find the stagnant pond where the old woman supposedly drowned all seven of her children.

I say her name three times. Nothing.

I reappear at the campfire, triumphant.

Everyone stares, fear slashed across their pimpled faces.

"What?" I say.

Behind me, a twig snaps.

DANA VICKERSON's work is forthcoming in *Zooscape* and *Dark Matter Presents: Human Monsters*. She's on Twitter @dmvickerson.

The Unknowable Awaits
Jameson Grey

It came from the stars – as old as the universe, as new as the earth.

It exists in the blink of an eye, the shifting of a continent, the precession of a galaxy, the pulse of an atom.

It stalks the day and lurks by night.

It crawls from within, from without.

It is here. For you.

You sense it at your back. You shiver, you tingle, your stomach curdles, your eyes twitch, your neck prickles. You turn – too slow, too late. You can never face it.

You don't know it, but it knows you.

It waited.

It is time.

JAMESON GREY's work has been published in numerous anthologies. He can be found online at jameson-grey.com and on Twitter @thejamesongrey.

Washed Ashore
Dorian J. Sinnott

They gathered at the lake when the beast washed ashore, gawking at the carcass rotting beneath the summer heat. It was at least the size of a barge, long neck twisted—tossed to the side. Gulls gathered at its mouth, picking away remnants of flesh stuck in its teeth.

The townsfolk couldn't help but feel relief as they stared. Knowing they were safe from encountering the creature on the lake. But out among the mist, the water churned, deep and dark—long neck breaking the surface. Far larger than the one washed ashore.

A desperate mother searching for her baby.

DORIAN J. SINNOTT's word has appeared in over 200 journals and has been nominated for the Best of the Net. Find him on Twitter @doriansinnott

A Dream of You
Gully Novaro

Every night I fall for the cruel trick my mind insists on playing. I dream of you and believe you are here.

Every morning I have to learn to live without you, when I wake up and you're not by my side.

It's exhausting, losing you every morning. Having to remember your death, relive my grief. I can't do it anymore. I won't.

When we get home I will wash you, dress you up in your pajamas, and put you to bed. When I wake up tomorrow, I will kiss your lips, it will be like you were never gone.

GULLY NOVARO is a non-binary writer from Argentina, with love for all things out of this world.

The Fog of War
Warren Benedetto

Jameson surveyed the battle-scarred landscape. Shadows rose from the mud, moving through the fog obscuring the carnage. The sharp smell of cordite hung in the air. Jameson's ears were numb — the only sound was the agonizing wail of an injured soldier on the ground beneath him. Shrapnel had shredded the man's face; his stomach was a gurgling pile of entrails. Jameson read the patch on the man's blood-soaked uniform. The name was familiar: T. Jameson.

His own.

Damn it, Jameson thought, recalling the whistling of the incoming mortar. *Direct hit.*

He sighed, then joined the other shadows in the fog.

"The Fog of War" was originally published in Dark Moments by Black Hare Press in September 2021.

WARREN BENEDETTO writes short fiction about horrible people doing horrible things. Visit www.warrenbenedetto.com and follow @warrenbenedetto on Twitter.

Inside
Michael Stroh

Melvin boarded up his doors and windows from the inside to keep them from breaking through. *It's not safe outside,* he thought, hammering steadily as darkness spread like ink between the cracks. He knew they were close. He glimpsed the family portrait on the mantle, felt the familiar strangling grief. He wouldn't let them kill again.

He pounded feverishly as they approached, first with ragged whispers, then they spoke his name, taunting.

Last board nailed tight, he dropped his hammer, hoping it was enough. That was the last thing he remembered before the voices grew louder still and took control.

MICHAEL STROH is a pastor and writer in the Dallas area. He and his wife Libby have three kids. Find him on Twitter @pastor_writer.

Skin

Kailey Alessi

I've always loved skin. How supple it is, stretching across fat and muscle and bone. It's endlessly moldable, really a perfect fabric. Most animals have skin that is much too thick, but human skin is perfect.

Hush, my dear.

As I was saying, skin is truly beautiful. Especially yours. It's so soft and clear, you really must tell me what kind of moisturizer you use.

Anyway, I am a bit of a collector. See that one? That was once a makeup influencer. Next to it was a dermatologist.

Oh, don't cry darling. I'll take good care of it for you.

KAILEY ALESSI has lived in Michigan and Idaho. An anthropology graduate student by day, by night she writes disturbing fiction.

The Lady of the Lake
Kai Delmas

"Sign says no fishing!"

Jake walks past Paul, down the dock. "Ain't nobody here to see us."

A low fog lies over the lake's surface. They cast their reels and wait.

"Ever hear of the lady of the lake?" Jake asks.

"From King Arthur?" Paul scratches his head.

"Nah. From this lake. She drifts through the fog when it rains. Protects nature and shit."

"Never heard of her." Paul sweats, eyes searching the ever-thickening fog.

"I got something." Jake starts reeling it in. "Something big."

It's a kayak. In it, a lady wearing a yellow raincoat with red glowing eyes.

KAI DELMAS loves creating worlds and magic systems and is a slush reader for Apex Magazine. He is a winner of the monthly *Apex* Microfiction Contest and his fiction can be found in *Martian* and is forthcoming in *Tree and Stone* and several Shacklebound anthologies. Find him on Twitter @KaiDelmas.

Das Medusenhaupt
Christopher Wood

"The dream of Medusa is a complex tapestry weaving sexuality, fear, and desire. The nightmares are your subconscious addressing your own castrated agency."

Dr. Perseo tapped the tip of his pen against his lips.

"But it's so real, I can feel...the movement, the power, the-"

Perseo sighed, "The nightmare is but a fantasy..."

The doctor's voice drifted as Euryale closed her eyes, manifesting the sensations from her dreams; the writhing of the snakes upon her head, the vastness of immortality. When she looked upon the room again Perseo's severed head hung from her fist, the dream a dream no more.

CHRISTOPHER WOOD lives in the UK with his wife and daughter. He is working on a collection of short stories.

The Guardian of Old
Jameson Grey

There were all sorts of stories suggesting the house was built on a geological fault or a deconsecrated graveyard or even a space-time rift. The spirit watching over the house was older than that – older than primordial soup. It had existed since before time, occasionally appearing, mostly to observe.

Now was not such a time.

As the world wept, the frequency of strange visitations increased, and the old house's occupants fled. There was nowhere distant enough for them to go. Humans hadn't even set foot on other planets yet.

The guardian of ancient Earth had awoken. And it was angry.

JAMESON GREY's work has been published in numerous anthologies. He can be found online at jameson-grey.com and on Twitter @thejamesongrey.

Low Tide
Joachim Heijndermans

The water recedes. Low tide is coming. With my last rope I bind leaves over the gash on my arm.

A wave crashes on the sand, exposing a pitch-black skull that I'd missed earlier. I throw it on the pile. Where is the rest of it? Even headless, they can still move. Poor Carrie learned that the hard way.

The sun is high. It's too beautiful a day to be in terror. My 'weapons', junk from the crash, are still good. But how many will come today?

A black skeleton emerges from the water, looking at me with furious hunger.

JOACHIM HEIJNDERMANS is a writer and artist from the Netherlands. His work is featured in SFFH magazines, podcasts, and animation.

Alpaca Lips
Chip Houser

"It's so pretty!" Tina said, pointing at the orange dome blooming over the neighbors' rooftops.

Her father pulled her off the swing and ran for the basement.

"I want to paint my room that color!" she said, pointing over his shoulder.

"Don't look," her father said, pressing her head to his chest.

"What is it, Daddy?" Tina said.

He stumbled over the quaking ground, trying to say, "It's the Apocalypse," but he stumbled over his words, too.

"The what-a lips?" she said.

"It doesn't matter—"

Before he could say the words that did matter, the blast wave hit them.

"Alpaca Lips" was first published in The Arcanist, November 2019.

CHIP HOUSER's short fiction has propagated across many genre and literary markets. Follow him @chazzlepants and find story links at chiphouser.com.

Lure
Cara Twomey

The mysterious figure caught his eye, and it beckoned to him. He wasn't going to follow. He knew he shouldn't. But something about it was so mesmerizing that he found he could not resist. There was something about it which lured him in its direction. He had to follow it.

He followed the mysterious, shadowy figure out of the light traveling further and further into darkness. Something in him told him he shouldn't go, but he had to. He was too drawn in to stop.

Then the mysterious, shadowy figure finally became clear, and he had no chance to run.

CARA TWOMEY is a writer and college student. Her Instagram is @c.v.twomey.

A Husband's Return
Toshiya Kamei

"You're home early, otonosama." Shizuka bowed, her kimono rustling. Her warrior husband stood in the gloom and stared at nothing. "When did you get back?" His armor looked frayed and rusted. Shizuka gasped at his chalk-white face.

He stepped outside. The hens shrieked, frantically flapping their wings. Shizuka grabbed a lantern and chased him into the yard. The dim light revealed a pool of blood beside the chicken coop. Shizuka hoped against hope that a famished fox was the culprit of the mess. Then lightning flashed, illuminating her husband's deathly figure. Blood gushed from a gaping hole in his chest.

"A Husband's Return" was originally published in Hundred Word Horror: Home in February 2021.

TOSHIYA KAMEI writes short fiction inspired by mythology, folklore, and fairy tales.

Black Site Detainees: Prisoner 27
Coby Rosser

"We need confirmation of death to remove remains."

"Any coroner can issue certificates. Even under hazmat. Why special request?"

"There's some debate as to whether this inmate is actually deceased."

"Elaborate."

"Attempting escape, he consumed mold off the back of his toilet to become sick and get moved into the medical ward. And well... Never mind. Here we are. Look for yourself."

Prisoner 27 laid upon his cot in a discolored mess of morbid obesity, distended and verrucose, with black, hirsute mold bursting from orifices. Slow chest aspirations produced a grayish miasma around his nostrils.

"He weighed ninety-six pounds—before."

COBY ROSSER is a Computer Analyst and May 2022 flash fiction contest winner at *Apparition Literary Magazine.*

Tweet him @paperninjaman

Countdown
E.S. Huberty

10, the text reads. Unknown number. The next day, *9*. A weird prank. A funky bot scam. The texts keep popping up. *8. 7.*

"What happens when they get to zero?" Axel asks, slurping his peach ice tea in a way that nauseates me. "Ask them."

Smiley face emoji, the stranger replies.

"So weird," Axel scoffs.

6. 5. Axel steals my turkey sandwich from the fridge. *4. 3.* He leaves his sweaty socks on my desk. *2.* He scrapes my car door. *1.*

I scrub Axel's blood from my fingernails as my phone's text alert chimes. *0. Thumb's up emoji.*

E.S. HUBERTY is a freelance writer, horror fan, and forest lover living outside Portland, Oregon.

The Chaos Gospel
Conrad Gardner

I hear them. My disciples. Singing my song. Their gospel.

Gathered in their robes or naked, donning makeup, they stand in my church. My loving disciples preach their dark sermon, screaming it from the bottom of their lungs, prayers to me travelling the air.

My influence crosses the land and touches the souls of people who hear. Those who obey know what they must do. They don their armour, worship at my altar. They open themselves to the essence of my children, true believers of my word.

Once they've offered themselves as sacrifice, it's time for beautiful chaos to spread.

CONRAD GARDNER's fiction has previously been published by *Martian Magazine*, *Black Ink Fiction*, and *A Thin Slice of Anxiety*. https://conradgardner.com/

Bowling
Mike Murphy

Dougie devoured his Cheerios. His mother attributed it to growing-boy hunger and a desire to get on with the weekend.

As Mom answered the doorbell, her boy noticed an odd bubbling in the milk remaining in the bowl. He stared momentarily and then poked at it with his teaspoon.

It happened so quickly, Dougie didn't think to let go of the spoon the cow spirits used to pull him – who couldn't make milk himself! – headfirst into the bowl, drowning him in the milk they had worked hard to produce and that he just wasted without a care in the world.

MIKE MURPHY's tales have been published in audio, prose, and film. See his blog [at audioauthor.blogspot.com] for his credits.

A Little Bit of Electricty
Alyson Tait

P ins and needles in my fingers wake me up. I try to wiggle my wrists to bring the blood back, but I'm tied down.

Wrists. Thighs. Feet. Chest. Neck.

There is even a strap around my forehead. Something sits on my scalp.

I blink, eyes heavy and cloudy from sleep. I don't even remember where I passed out and don't know where I woke up.

When my vision clears, I see a man.

A man with a yellow grin, whose hand is on a lever with wires that match the ones on my chair.

He pulls downward.

And he laughs.

ALYSON TAIT has appeared in *(mac)ro(mic)* and *Wrongdoing Magazine*, among others. You can find her on Twitter @rudexvirus1 or at AlysonTait.com.

Watch Where You Go
Marie Claire Sawa

The wide-jawed monster waits across inconspicuous gaps in everyday life.

On the wrong side of a utility pole in a dusked alley. In one square of the jungle gym kids climb on a sunny summer day. Inside the car door you swing open while watching your phone screen.

Without right or wrong, good or bad, the red-mouthed calamity sits, eager to embrace. Crunching on a hapless pigeon that flutters into its gape, it longs for bigger prey.

So watch where you go. Next time you raise your gaze, hot breath and bloody teeth may be right in front of you.

MARIE CLAIRE SAWA writes marketing copy for writing & publishing businesses by day and horror by night. Say hello on Twitter @MarieCSawa.

Haunting
Michael Stroh

Daphne screams. I keep haunting her by mistake. She must have glimpsed me in the kitchen window's reflection, nothing more than a whisper of presence behind her. She turns in panic and now she looks right through me. For a moment I wonder and even hope as her eyes search, then pause where I stand, but she only shakes her head and laughs at herself.

She still wears her ring. I want her to know I haven't left her, but I can only frighten her. I see my faded reflection in the glass, so I step aside, out of sight.

MICHAEL STROH is a pastor and writer in the Dallas area. He and his wife Libby have three kids. Find him on Twitter @pastor_writer.

Once They Are In

Simeon Care

Throughout time, across the world, they have been. The slow, gnawing fears, the harmful thoughts, the inner demons. Leaking in and ruining our minds, like wood smoke into fresh linen.

A darkening of thought, a sensation of doubt, a sinking feeling in the gut; these are the tell-tale signs that one of these hell-spawn black worms has burrowed in and taken hold.

Once they are in, they are impossible to remove. Impossible to kill.

Tenebris cogitationes nunc—the words of summoning, of death. Read them at your peril and know your fate is sealed.

Blackness will come upon you shortly.

SIMEON CARE is an English writer, specialising in speculative fiction and horror. For more stories please see his website.

Call

Don Money

Grandpa told me of the cave he found in the hills behind the farm. When he was a boy something called to him from it. He entered but was afraid to go deeper into the darkness. The voice was ragged and cut furrows across his brain like a plow, so he ran.

The cave now stands before me, the call bouncing around my head. I know what it whispers must be lies, but the promises of this elder god resonates within me. I crawl inside until a tentacle wraps around me to bring me to the power I so crave.

DON MONEY writes stories across a variety of genres. His stories have appeared in a variety of anthologies and magazines.

Returned and Taken
Don Money

"Where are my missing body parts?" I asked the man standing over my dead body on the gurney. He wore a gray three piece suit covered in splatters of blood.

He tilted his head upward in the direction of where I floated, shocked to see my ghostly form over him. The scalpel he held suddenly was pointed in my direction in his fearful attempt to ward me off.

The long incision across my abdomen, the bloody detritus of my internals laying on a stainless steel tray told the story.

"Gone," he stammered.

"I guess yours will have to do then."

DON MONEY writes stories across a variety of genres. His stories have appeared in a variety of anthologies and magazines.

Yo Ho Ho
Joachim Heijndermans

Mutineers. They take me ship and me gold. Shot me thrice in the belly, cut me throat, then threw me overboard. Bastards. Should've cut me to pieces.

Don't know how still walk as I'm nothing but bones. No matter. I got me cutlass and me legs. And I know where they'll be docking me ship.

I'll walk across this wet desert till I reach the buccaneer harbor in Crescent Cove, hidden from the royals and Spanish. Where their homes, their wives and their children be. I will have me fun, then wait till those bastards come home.

Yo ho ho.

"Yo Ho Ho" was previously published in the Black Hare Press anthology
OCEANS.

JOACHIM HEIJNDERMANS is a writer and artist from the Netherlands. His work is featured in SFFH magazines, podcasts, and animation.

Repossession
Rachel L. Tilley

Twisted curls loop round my finger. With every gesture, the vines close in a little more tightly. They attempt to spring back, recoiling as they meet resistance, but I force them inwards; embrace you a little more.

For the moment you're subsisting. Your apathetic heart is still beating.

I have to constrict it; choke it.

It must not be allowed to persist – misguided, misdirected.

Squeezing my fist... I cannot bring myself to take that final drop of life.

The pain in your eyes reflects my own.

But when you open your mouth to speak, I know I cannot let you.

RACHEL L. TILLEY, who lives in the UK, writes short stories in the fantasy and horror genres. www.instagram.com/rachel_l_tilley

Below The Depths
Conrad Gardner

We were told to look for The Maria, her treasure. That's all.

Going a few thousand feet under the surface, it wasn't the lung pressure I was scared of. It was what I saw out there. No monsters. Just them. The ones who went down with their ships. Captains, most of them.

They called out for me, the ones on the *Maria*. Asked me for help. Grabbed me. Communications to the boat went down. I didn't say anything anyway. I was busy screaming.

They'll be looking for me soon. But I have a new crew now. And we aren't recruiting.

CONRAD GARDNER's fiction has previously been published by *Martian Magazine, Black Ink Fiction,* and *A Thin Slice of Anxiety.* https://conradgardner.com/

Christmas Truce
Eric Lewis

John and Heinrich looked across fields of overgrown trenches and mortar holes. "Here we are again. Another year passed."

"We never left," said his old enemy, "not really."

"I know. The battlefield's almost unchanged."

"It's no memorial!" Heinrich insisted. "Quite the opposite. They want to leave it be, forget entirely."

"Can't blame them, so do I. Except Christmas. Our truce. Remember, we played football, traded cigarettes?"

"I remember. Officers were furious. Next day, right back to it."

"The last day."

At sunrise two dead soldiers disappeared into the air for another year, though never to leave the place. Not really.

"Christmas Truce" originally appeared in The Black Hare Press anthology Beyond: Dark Drabbles #4, published in September 2019.

ERIC LEWIS is the author of *The Heron Kings* series and multiple works of short speculative fiction. Visit ericlewis.ink

On an Open Fire
Mike Murphy

They were making fun of him!

Derek read the incantation in the dusty book over the matches, struck one, and touched the flame to the holiday card. It burned slowly, the now-animated family in the photo terrified. Confined to their four-sided paper prison, they would die.

He smiled as the card crackled in the barrel. He could see the real fire in his mind.

Derek had no wife or kids, but did he need to be reminded of that every December?

Uncle Trevor's family wouldn't mock him next Christmas, and there were more matches for anybody else who dared try.

"On an Open Fire" was originally published in December 2019 by Tales from the Moonlit Path.

MIKE MURPHY's tales have been published in audio, prose, and film. See his blog [at audioauthor.blogspot.com] for his credits.

The Whaler and the Whale
Larry Hodges

"You're supposed to try to escape," Jim exclaimed, "not surface right in front of our harpoon cannon!" Other whalers were already aiming the harpoons. Soon they'd tear into the flesh of this silly humpback whale.

Why? The thought whispered in his mind.

"Who said that?" he cried. The whale turned sideways and stared at him with one of its surprisingly small, dark eyes. "Really—you? Because we need to make a living."

Oh.

Suddenly dizzy, he grabbed a railing. Everything went wet. He saw the man—*himself!*—staring down at him from the ship. Then the first harpoons hit.

Sorry.

LARRY HODGES has sold over 130 stories and four novels, and claims he's the world's best ping-pong playing writer.

A Local's Guide on What to Do and Not Do for Halloween in Salem, Massachusetts

Steve Zisson

DON'T go to the Salem Witch Museum. Historically inaccurate.

DON'T go to the Salem Wax Museum. Wax museums are the very definition of fake.

DON'T look for where witches were burned. None were burned; most were hanged.

DON'T go on guided tours claiming to know haunted places. They've no idea where Salem's ghosts are.

DO go to the dark tunnel under Greenlawn Cemetery. There'll be a faint light through the creaky gate down the stairs. You'll become claustrophobic. You'll scream! There'll be blood, including yours.

Brought to you by the local, tentacled being lurking in the tunnel beneath Greenlawn Cemetery.

STEVE ZISSON's fiction appears in *Daily Science Fiction, Nature's Future, Little Blue Marble,* among others. He grew up in Salem.

An Ocean of Souls
Addison Smith

Voices call beneath the waves of waving starlight and jellyfish ribbons. My knees press into the sodden wood of my dinghy and I reach through the water's surface.

Her face is there, clever Desdemona in all her beauty. I brush my hand across her cheek and she smiles radiant as the moon.

Tears trickle down my face. "Do not be sad," she says. "This is my home now."

I look past the rope burns around her neck. In the ocean of souls, we see only what we wish to see.

I slip into the water and lay by her side.

ADDISON SMITH wants to talk to you. No, really! You can find him on Twitter @AddisonCSmith.

Your Biggest Fan
Conrad Gardner

You're my dream. Like an inflatable doll. I love seeing your latex-bound stomach expand and flatten as you move, singing your heart out. You don't know I'm watching you, but I'm at every concert.

On-stage, you stand there in your tight leather skirts and your thigh-high boots. Sung from your lips, your music is like honey on the tongue. But the noise I enjoy best is the squeak your trousers made when I grabbed you. Not a squeak. A squeal. They made a beautiful sound. Your skin's smooth, like vinyl.

Now, here, in your cage, your new stage, sing for me.

CONRAD GARDNER's fiction has previously been published by *Martian Magazine*, *Black Ink Fiction*, and *A Thin Slice of Anxiety*. https://conradgardner.com/

Sacrifices
Jim Anderson

The path ran through a clearing in the woods, ferns on either side as tall as me. Beyond the clearing, a swamp. The path died in a rotted log.

That's where I left my sacrifices — trading cards, pencils, rubber balls. A pair of pink tennis shoes I found in the woods. I'd place them on the log and make a wish. "I'd like an 'A' on my test, please." I always got the grade or one close enough. The sacrifices disappeared.

Important stuff worked best.

To take care of Bernie the Bully, I left my Spider-Man comics.

All of them.

JIM ANDERSON lives in southeast Michigan, USA. See more of his micro-fiction at JimTheWriter.net.

Conquest
Roger Johns

Their nearly odorless pheromones are instant paralytics, but I can still *feel* them, those plump little slugs that drop onto my face from that hole in the ceiling above my bunk, then ooze with impunity across my eyes and lips, throbbing gently against the insides of my nostrils as they burrow into my frontal sinuses. They pack tightly within those warm moist cavities, less than an inch from my brain, inducing a fitful slumber. When the delta waves from deep sleep begin to dissipate, they will exit, but until then, their vile thoughts of total conquest will dominate my dreams.

ROGER JOHNS is the author of the *Wallace Hartman Mysteries* and a 2018 Georgia Author of the Year.

The Copyediting of a Typo-Strewn Apocalyptic Novel

J. J. Steinfeld

As the middle-aged copyeditor stared at her work monitor, the last chapter of a typo-strewn apocalyptic novel set in her home town, the text was replaced by a photograph of her entering her house as a meteorite struck. She tried to return to copyediting, but each time she touched the keyboard, a voice warned, "Do not go home tonight..."

She was the last one left in the office, but the photograph and voice convinced her to stay.

The newspaper thrown onto her front porch the next day had a shocking headline: METEORITE STRIKES OFFICE BUILDING. ONE BODY FOUND IN RUBBLE.

The Copyediting of a Typo-Strewn Apocalyptic Novel" was first published in Drabble Harvest #7, September 2016.

CANADIAN **J.J. Steinfeld** has published 23 books, including *Somewhat Absurd, Somehow Existential* (Poetry/Guernica Editions/2021), *Acting on the Island* (Stories/Pottersfield Press/2022).

In Dreams I Walk With You
Mel Reynes

I softly whisper a silent prayer in your sleeping ear, just enough to send you dreams. Sweet dreams of the time we'll spend and the things we'll build—a home, a family, a life.

And then I leave forever, slipping out the door to my waiting starship. I silently promise to hold your name close to mine in my third, most special, heart.

As we consume your species' flesh, I'll whisper it to myself.

As we strip mine your earth, I'll compose it into songs.

As we conquer the galaxy, your name will be on a thousand lips, my immortal love.

MEL REYNES writes horror and science fiction about the fantastical terror of living in the early 21st century. Mel is afraid of the woods, frogs, biking at night, and using her phone. Mel has two spooky cats and enjoys living in Rhode Island. If you ever meet Mel in real life, offer her a tasty duck and run away.

Parasitic Apparition
H.V. Patterson

D r. Jackson's colleagues didn't see any rash. They ran blood tests and claimed she was healthy, no trace of internal parasites.

But she could feel them leeching the iron from her blood, could see the angry furrows they left beneath her skin as they bore through her, up her legs, her torso, inching their way to her brain.

Then, they were inside her head, the ghosts of all the nematodes she'd eradicated from her patients.

She staggered, dizzy from Albenza. Screaming, hands curled to fists, she pounded at her skull, desperate to silence the chewing of a million spectral jaws.

H.V. PATTERSON loves horror, the supernatural, and the dark side of science. Follow her on Twitter: @ScaryShelley

Moving Onward
Kelas Lloyd

The fog is an obvious obstacle, hanging low in the valley where it shouldn't be. The optimist would call it cover. They would probably be right; it just wouldn't be cover for them. There is, of course, no other way to go. Behind them the kinnyebreeth march, behemoths whose favorite meal is bone marrow. To the west are deadly swamps, the east holds the nightsirens, which means the only way left is forward.

Three minutes after they enter the fog the screams begin, mixed with pleas for mercy. Seven minutes later the valley is silent again.

The fog moves on.

KELAS LLOYD is a disabled and queer artist, author, and cat lover working to survive Texas. They're on Twitter @Tandadader

Don't miss out!

Visit the website below and you can sign up to receive emails whenever Eric Fomley publishes a new book. There's no charge and no obligation.

https://books2read.com/r/B-A-PMCT-APHBC